EGMONT
We bring stories to life

First published in Great Britain in 2009 by Egmont UK Limited,
239 Kensington High Street, London W8 6SA

Editor: Sally Gilbert
Designer: Laura Bird
Photography: Laura Ashman

ISBN 978 1 4052 4647 7
1 3 5 7 9 10 8 6 4 2
Printed in Italy

Note to parents: adult supervision is recommended when sharp-pointed items such as scissors are in use.

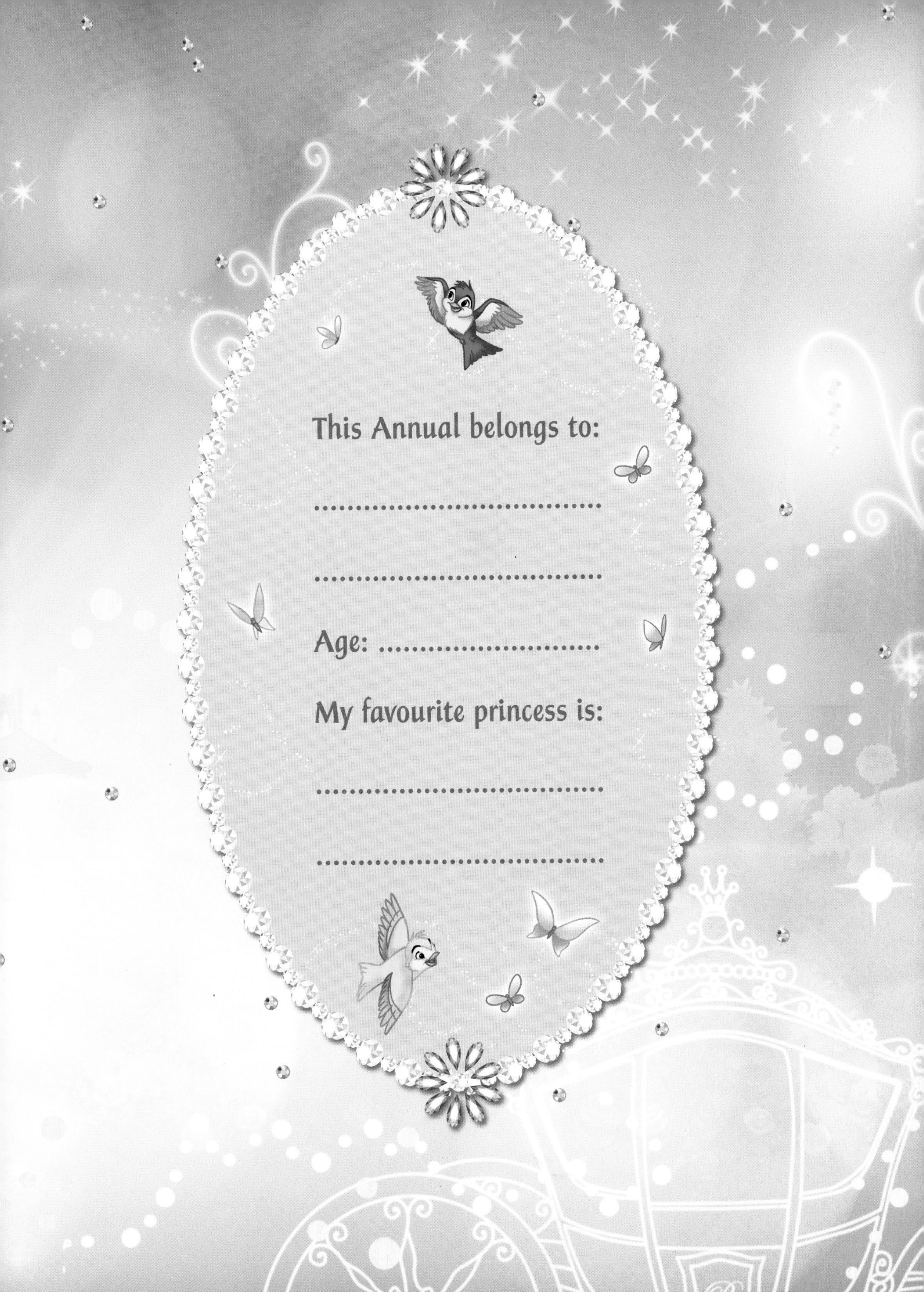
This Annual belongs to:
....
....
Age: ....
My favourite princess is:
....
....

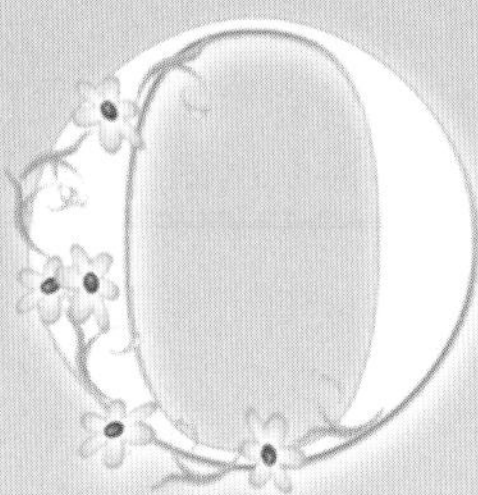

Once upon a time, in fairy-tale kingdoms far away, there lived six beautiful princesses...

Contents

Cinderella

Cinderella Factfile

Description: True fairy–tale princess.

Hair: Blonde and flowing.

Eyes: Clear blue and as deep as the ocean.

Friends: The mice, who help her with her daily chores.
The Fairy Godmother, who is her magical friend.

Personality: Hardworking and positive.

Romance: Prince Charming.

Royal Portrait

Read my secret palace diary.

Dear Diary,
Today there was a special occasion at the palace and I was very excited. I spent extra time in my dressing-room making sure I looked princess-perfect!

Gus said I looked beautiful, which was very sweet of him and Jaq, as inquisitive as ever, wanted to know why I was making such an extra special effort.

So, I told them that a royal artist was visiting the palace to paint my portrait that very afternoon and I needed to add lots of extra princess touches to look my very best.

Gus and Jaq were delighted – they loved the portraits on the palace walls. They would often spend time looking at all the kings, queens, princes and princesses of days gone by. In fact, they liked portraits so much that Jaq asked, "Can we be in it, too, Cinderella?"

How could I refuse my best friends? It would be difficult.

"I don't think mice are allowed in royal portraits," I told them tactfully, "but I'll ask the Grand Duke."

Later, when I asked the Grand

Duke, he was flabbergasted. "Mice?" he blustered. "In your official royal portrait? Ridiculous!"

When I returned to my dressing room, I had an idea. "Perhaps there is a way for my friends to be in the picture, too," I thought, and I searched through my jewellery box for my special locket.

When I arrived at the grand sitting room, the artist was waiting for me with his easel set up. He asked me to sit quite still in the seat - which was very difficult! I tried not to giggle!

"Make sure you get my locket in," I told the artist. "It was a present from the Prince."

He promised me he would get every detail into the painting.

When the artist had finished, he showed everyone my royal portrait.

He had included the locket, as promised. So, if you look at the painting closely, you will see that inside the locket there is a picture of Gus and Jaq, my very best friends!

Lots of love
from
Cinderella

Tiara Match

Can you match the pairs of tiaras, then find the odd one out?

Answer: the pairs of tiaras are 1 and 4, 2 and 5, 3 and 7. 6 is the odd one out.

Ballgown Magic

Look at the scene below and decide if the following statements are True or False.

1 The Fairy Godmother is waving her magic pencil.

True ♡ or False ♡

2 Cinderella's dress is pale pink.

True ♡ or False ♡

3 Cinderella's hair is blonde.

True ♡ or False ♡

4 There are two mice watching Cinderella and the Fairy Godmother.

True ♡ or False ♡

Answers: 1 false, she is waving her magic wand, 2 false, Cinderella's dress is pale blue, 3 true, 4 false, there are 3 mice watching Cinderella and the Fairy Godmother.

Cinderella Colouring

Heart Handbag

Make and use this heart handbag for a princess ball.

You will need:

paper bag

silver paper

pink card

safety scissors

glue

glitter glue

1

Cover a paper bag with silver paper and glue it down. Fold the top oven to make a flap, then fold and glue the corners under, as shown.

2

Cut out some hearts from pink card. Decorate each one with glitter glue. Leave the hearts to dry.

3

Stick the hearts on to the bag and decorate further with glitter glue. You can fasten the bag with sticky tack or a ribbon if you wish.

Jasmine

Jasmine Factfile

Description: Daughter of the powerful Sultan.

Hair: Black, tied with jewelled bands and ribbons.

Eyes: Almond–shaped, brown and deep.

Friends: Rajah, her faithful pet tiger and Abu, the monkey.

Personality: An adventurous dreamer.

Romance: Aladdin.

Magic Island

1 One day, Jasmine and Aladdin were putting the finishing touches to a royal parade. "Oh, dear! I have been looking forward to this parade for so long," sneezed the Sultan, "but I don't think I will be well enough to attend."

2 Jasmine felt sorry for her father. "I wish I could make him feel better in time," she said to Aladdin. "Let's go and visit this magical doctor I know," suggested Aladdin.

3 Jasmine agreed but she was worried about leaving her father. "We are just going out for a short while, Father," Jasmine said. "We will be back soon."

4 Jasmine and Aladdin flew straight to the doctor to ask for some medicine for the Sultan. "I am afraid that no medicine exists," explained the doctor, "but . . .

5 ". . . I do know of a magical island where you may find a cure. Here is a map and necklace to help you. Good luck, Jasmine," the doctor said.

6 Jasmine and Aladdin flew to 'Magic Island' on the Magic Carpet, using the map. "There it is," said Aladdin, pointing into the distance.

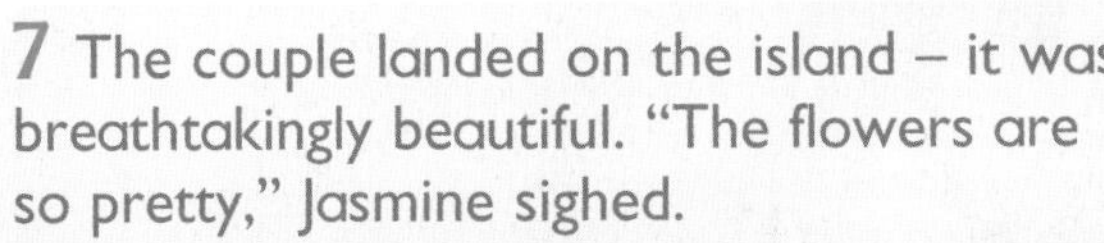

7 The couple landed on the island – it was breathtakingly beautiful. "The flowers are so pretty," Jasmine sighed.

8 Just then, the necklace the doctor had given Jasmine caught on a twig and fell into a stream.

9 Suddenly, there was a gigantic explosion and the Sultan's poorly face appeared before them.

10 Poor Aladdin was flung into a nearby bush by the force of the explosion. Then, a bottle appeared in Jasmine's hand. "Try rubbing the bottle, Jasmine," Aladdin called, "it may be magic!"

11 Jasmine rubbed the bottle and sure enough three princess genies appeared. "Hi, Jasmine! We can grant you any wish you like," they said, giggling.

12 "I wish that my father was well enough for the parade," Jasmine said. "Your wish is granted," one of the princess genies said, "but you must reach your father before the sun sets."

13 So Jasmine and Aladdin hurried back to the palace before the sun set. "I hope you like the flowers I picked for you," Aladdin said. "So romantic," Jasmine replied.

14 Back at the palace, Jasmine and Aladdin found the Sultan back to his old self. "I feel much better," the Sultan smiled. "I can't wait for the parade tomorrow."

15 The royal parade was lots of fun and everyone had a great time. "Father is as fit as he has been in years," said Jasmine, dancing, "I can hardly keep up with him!"

The End

Romantic Day

Love is in the air for Jasmine and Aladdin.

These small pictures are jumbled up.

Which two swaps will make them match the big picture below?

a b  c

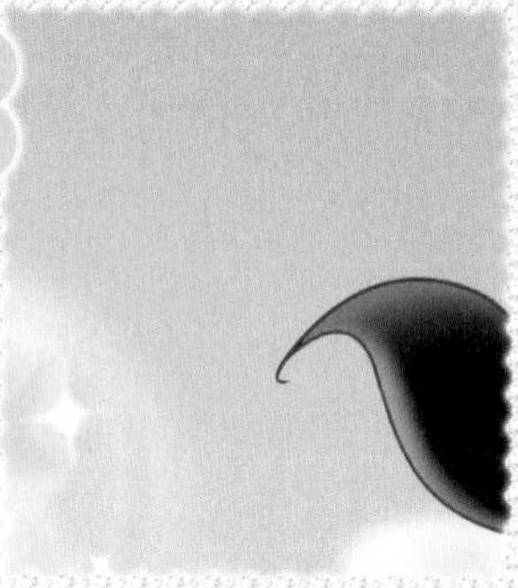

d  e  f

Answers: you need to swap c and b and d and e.

Jasmine Colouring

Lucky Lamp

Play this game with a friend and see if your three wishes will be granted.

How to play

Take turns to throw a dice. If the number beside one of your wishes is thrown, tick it off. The first player to tick off all three of their wishes is the winner!

Flower Sash

Make Jasmine's flower sash – it will add sparkle to any outfit.

You will need:

- squares of felt
- ribbon
- glitter glue
- safety scissors
- glue

1 Cut a length of ribbon long enough to make a sash. Cut out flower shapes from the pink and yellow felt.

2 Decorate the flowers with glitter glue. Stick them on to the ribbon when they are dry. Ask an adult to tie the sash loosely around your body.

Belle

Belle Factfile

Description: A beautiful French maiden.

Hair: Brown, tied back with a pretty ribbon.

Eyes: Big, brown and velvety.

Friends: The Enchanted Objects: Lumiere, Cogsworth, Mrs Potts and Chip.

Personality: A true romantic with a kind heart.

Romance: The Beast.

The Big Surprise

Read my diary entry about the Beast's party.

Dear Diary,

Recently, the Beast has been so grumpy, that the Enchanted Objects and I decided to arrange a surprise party to cheer him up.

It was really difficult to keep the party a secret, because the Beast is so nosy!

Today, I was making a new ballgown for the party and the Beast came over and said, "What are you making?"

"I'm just practising a new sewing stitch," I replied, thinking quickly.

Next, Mrs Potts told me that the Beast had found her making a delicious cake for the party.

"Why are you baking a cake?" he asked her.

"I'm just practising a new recipe," said Mrs Potts, as she hid the party candles.

Later, Cogsworth told me that when the Beast left the kitchen, a balloon floated past him. "Um, we're practising blowing up balloons," Cogsworth told him.

The Beast noticed that Lumiere was lighting lots of candles, too. "I'm just practising for when it gets dark," Lumiere told the Beast.

The Beast must have thought our behaviour was very odd and it put him in a really, really bad mood.

"Maybe I should go off and practise something myself," he said, sulkily.

Anyway, that evening, when the party was ready, I couldn't find the Beast

anywhere. I then heard banging noises coming from the far end of the garden. When I got there, I found that the Beast had been busy himself, practising his woodwork.

When I led the Beast to the ballroom, everything suddenly made perfect sense to him; I was wearing my new party gown, the ballroom was decorated with balloons and Lumiere was lighting the candles on Mrs Potts' cake.

"Surprise!" we all shouted. "We wanted to have a party to cheer you up!"

"Where have you been?" asked Chip. "We've been waiting ages for you."

The Beast smiled and placed the cake on a beautiful cake stand he had made. "I've been practising my woodwork!" he laughed. The Beast never fails to surprise me! He can be ever so sweet sometimes.

Lots of love from

Belle

Feathered Friends

How many of Belle's birds can you count? Write the number in the heart.

How many pink flowers can you count? Write the number in the flower.

Answers: There are 6 birds and 8 pink flowers.

Magical Rose

Belle's magical rose can see the future.

Choose a question from the rose-wheel. Then throw a coin or button on to the roses at the bottom of the page to get your answer.

Will I learn to ride a horse?

Will I travel far?

Will I fall in love?

Will I be rich?

Will I have an adventure?

Will I marry a prince?

Yes

No

Maybe

Belle Colouring

These pictures look the same but there are three things missing in picture 2. Draw them back in and then colour the whole picture using picture 1 as a guide.

Answers: The three things missing from picture 2 are: the Beast's tail, the bow from the Beast's hair and part of the swag on Belle's gown.

Belle *Hairstyle*

Follow these steps for beautiful Belle hair!

1 Brush your hair and then pull it back into a ponytail.

2 Twist the ponytail into a bun and secure in place with hair pins.

3 Finally, add a pretty fabric rose to the bun and you will look as beautiful as a princess.

Princess Tip:

Try fixing small rose clips into the front of your hair, too.

Snow White

Snow White Factfile

Description: A princess through and through.

Hair: Black, with a pretty red hair band.

Eyes: Soft, gentle brown.

Friends: The Seven Dwarfs and the many forest creatures.

Personality: Sweet, graceful and naive.

Romance: The Prince.

Rainbow Day

1 One day, Snow White and the Prince had been for a romantic ride in the forest and they decided to stop by the dwarfs' cottage on their way home. "We saw the most wonderful rainbow today," Snow White told the dwarfs.

2 "But I forgot to make a wish and you should always wish on a rainbow!" she sighed, sadly.

3 The dwarfs asked the Prince to bring Snow White to the diamond mine tomorrow. "We have a surprise for her," they said.

4 When the Prince agreed, the dwarfs grabbed their tools and rushed off to the diamond mine. "How very odd," thought Snow White, as she waved them goodbye.

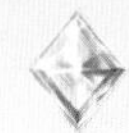

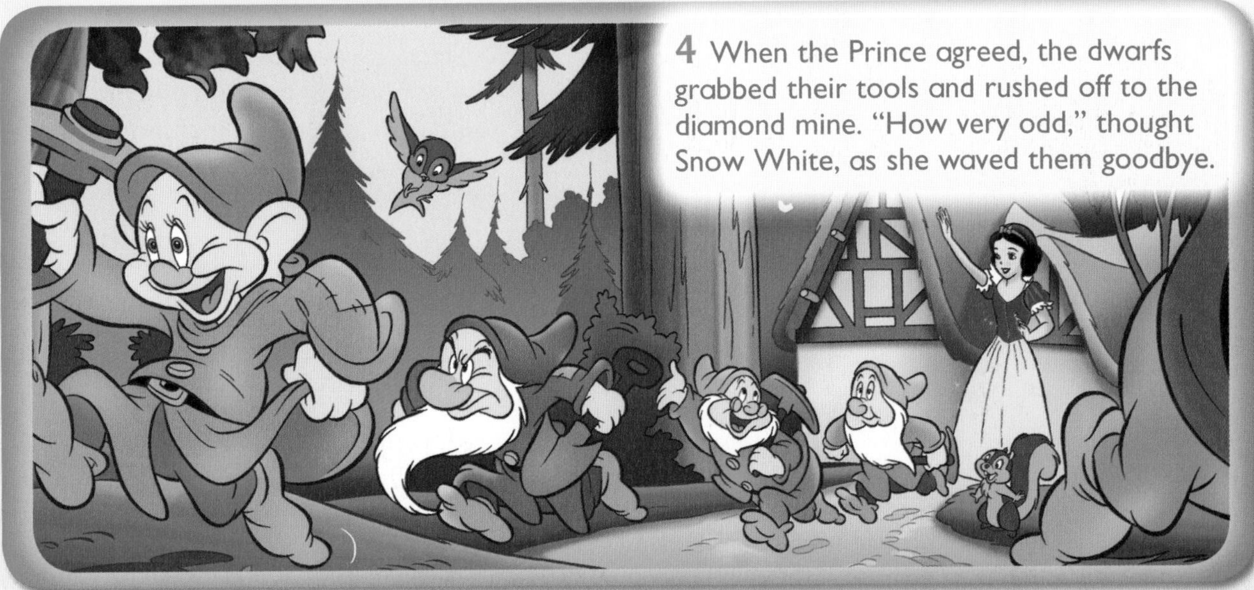

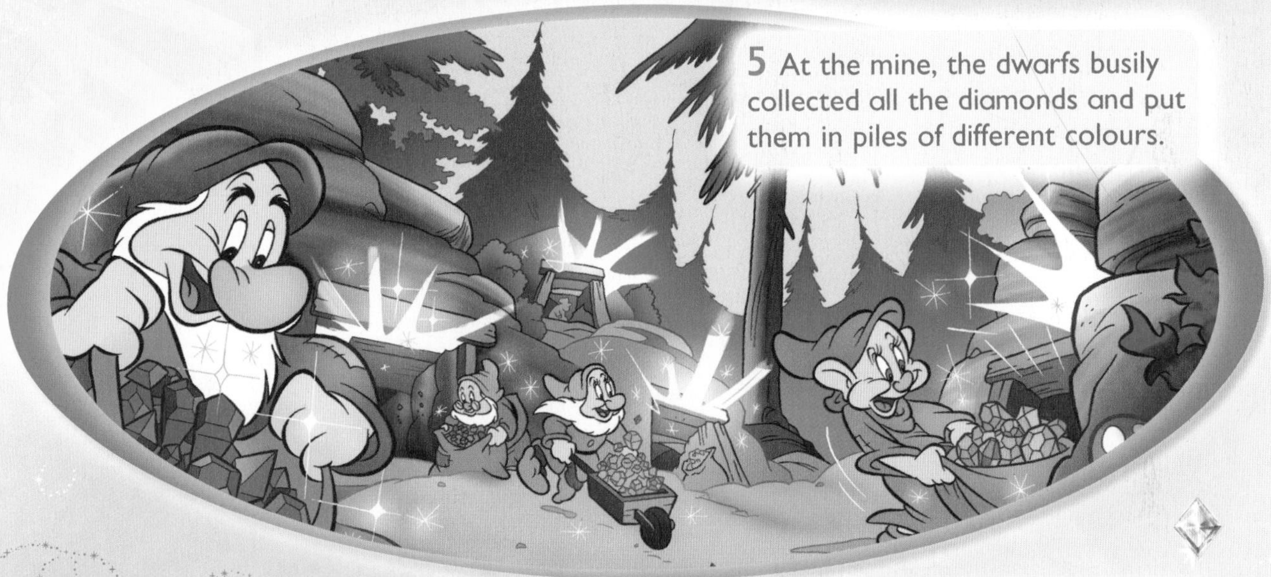

5 At the mine, the dwarfs busily collected all the diamonds and put them in piles of different colours.

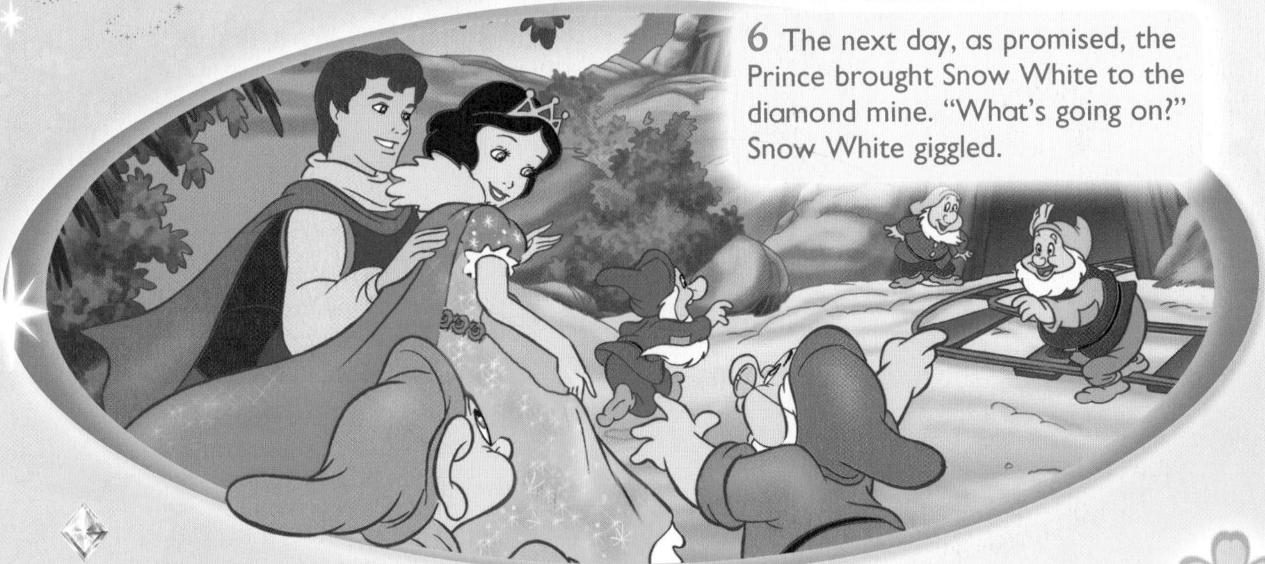

6 The next day, as promised, the Prince brought Snow White to the diamond mine. "What's going on?" Snow White giggled.

7 The dwarfs ran off and came back, each holding a piece of jewellery. "Every piece is a different colour of the rainbow," they said, proudly.

8 "How sweet, thank you!" Snow White blushed, as the dwarfs put the pieces of jewellery on her.

9 "Maybe you can make a wish now you are wearing all the colours of the rainbow," said Doc. "I wish I could," sighed Snow White, sweetly.

10 Later, back at the mine, Grumpy called a meeting. "Snow White is so sweet and kind but I still feel she is upset about the rainbow, so I have an idea," he said.

11 So, the next morning, bright and early, the dwarfs loaded their cart with diamonds and headed off. "Heigh-ho, heigh-ho," they sang.

12 Later, when Snow White awoke at the palace, there was something sparkling on the lawn right outside her bedroom window. "It's a rainbow!" she cried, delightedly.

13 She quickly got dressed and ran into the garden. "We made you this diamond rainbow, so you can make a wish under it," Grumpy said. "Thank you!" Snow White said, and wished. But she never said what she wished for because dreams don't come true if you tell, do they?

The End

Nature Notes

Snow White loves rabbits and she wants to tell you some interesting facts about them. Can you find the baby rabbit?

Rabbits love to twitch their nose – it's one of their ways of talking to each other.

Mummy rabbits are called does, daddy rabbits are called bucks and baby rabbits are called kits.

When rabbits are happy, they will jump and twist. This is called a binky.

Answers: The baby rabbit is hiding behind Snow White's cloak.

Draw Snow White

Snow White is walking in the palace garden.

Draw over the lines to finish picture 2, then colour it in using picture 1 as a guide.

1

2

Princess Makeover

Snow White would like a new look for a special occasion. Have fun playing this game on your own or with a friend.

How to play

You will need: Coloured pens or pencils and a coin.

Start at section '1' of Snow White's gown. To find out what colour it should be, close your eyes and drop a coin on to the coloured hearts. Colour the section of Snow White's gown in the same colour as the heart you have landed closest to. Carry on until you have coloured in all of Snow White's gown.

midnight blue

petal pink

apple red

berry purple

daffodil yellow

Princess Frame

Make Snow White's princess frame for your favourite picture.

You will need:

card

safety scissors

cotton wool

felt

glue

glitter glue

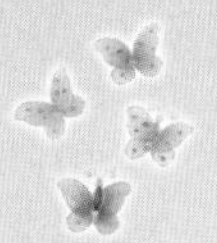

decoration

1. Take a rectangle of card and cut out a smaller rectangle, to make a frame. Glue cotton wool on to the frame.

2. Cover the cotton wool frame by neatly gluing felt over it. Decorate further by sticking on butterfly decorations and adding glitter glue. Finally, place your favourite princess picture behind the frame.

Ariel

Ariel Factfile

Description: A beautiful mermaid and the daughter of King Triton.

Hair: Long and fiery red.

Eyes: Bluish-green, like the sea.

Friends: Flounder the fish, Sebastian the crab and her six sisters.

Personality: Confident and curious.

Romance: Prince Eric.

The Ghost Ship

Read my diary entry about my adventures.

Dear Diary,
Today my sisters and I were feeling a little bored and we were thinking up new games to play.

"Let's tell each other ghost stories," my sister, Adella, suggested.

"I know where there is a REAL ghost!" Aquata told us. "The Haunted Ship at Folly Reef!"

"Come on," I said to my friends, Flounder and Sebastian the next day. "Let's go to Folly Reef and have an adventure!"

We soon spotted the haunted ship and swam in through a window.

"Who is that behind you?" squeaked Flounder, pointing in my direction.

"It won't work, silly!" I told him. "There are no ghosts here!"

Just then, I felt a hand on my shoulder and I looked around. Standing behind me was a beautiful ghost!

"You scared me. Who are you?" I gasped.

"I'm Celeste," she told me. "I am looking for my lost portrait, so I can break the curse and leave here."

"Well, we can help you," I said. "When did you last see it?"

"A very long time ago," Celeste smiled.

"Let's look in the bedchambers first," I suggested. We threw open an old wardrobe and found some beautiful gowns but no portrait in sight.

"Let's try the gowns on," said Celeste, dressing me up in a gown.

"Perhaps the portrait is in here?" Sebastian asked, pointing towards a chest. Opening the lid, Celeste looked

inside and found jewels but still no portrait. "These jewels would complement your gown perfectly," Celeste said, as she handed me a bracelet and earrings.

"One more try?" I suggested, and raced to pull back a curtain. Behind it, was a golden mirror.

"You look beautiful, Ariel," Flounder told me, as Celeste and I looked in the mirror together.

At that very moment, an incredible thing happened – a portrait appeared in the mirror's reflection, on the wall behind us!

"Your portrait!" I gasped. "We've broken the curse!"

Before our eyes, Celeste rose magically from the seabed towards the surface of the sea.

"Celeste!" I called and raced after her.

Breaking the surface, I saw Celeste on the ship's deck, waving to me.

"Thank you, Ariel, my heart is now free to go home. May your heart always be true, wherever you roam!" she said.

Suddenly, the ship shimmered in the sunlight, before fading into nothing.

That was the most amazing adventure I have ever had. And an adventure that is for your eyes only, diary.

Lots of love from Ariel

Bubble Trouble

Ariel is picking sea-flowers and dreaming of her prince.

These pictures look the same but four things are different in picture 2.
Colour in a bubble when you spot each one.

Answers: The sea-flower in Ariel's hand has changed colour, Sebastian has appeared, Flounder has appeared and a sea-flower has disappeared.

Princess Close-ups

What has Ariel seen on her adventures? Can you guess from the clues below?

1

They are aquatic mammals that are related to whales.

2

This fish is colourful and lives among sea anemones.

3

This sea creature has flippers and likes to eat fish.

4

This reptile likes to live in the sea. It has a hard shell like a tortoise.

Ariel Colouring

Ariel is searching for treasure. Colour in the picture as neatly as you can. How many shipwrecks can you count?
Answer: there are 3 shipwrecks.

Ocean Tiara

Make this pretty tiara to become a true ocean princess.

You will need:

glitter card

safety scissors

tape

sequins

glue

fine glitter

1 Cut out a strip from the glitter card to make a band to fit around your head. Also cut out some diamond shapes of different sizes, as shown.

2 Glue the diamond shapes on to the band, placing the biggest one in the middle.

3 Decorate the tiara with sequins and glitter, then glue and leave to dry. Bend the band into a circle and secure with tape. Crown yourself the newest princess of the ocean!

Aurora

Aurora Factfile

Description: Born into a royal family and betrothed to Prince Phillip.

Hair: Long and golden.

Eyes: Sparkling sapphire blue.

Friends: The good fairies and the woodland animals.

Personality: Very romantic and she loves to sing.

Romance: Prince Phillip.

Aurora's Banquet

1 One day, Aurora was visiting her Fairy Godmothers at their cottage in the forest. "What are you doing today?" Aurora asked them. "We're making new magical potions," Flora replied.

2 After a while, Aurora had to leave her friends. "I have to host a banquet at the palace tonight," Aurora explained, "so put a good luck spell on it for me."

3 But on her return to the palace, Aurora discovered that all the people preparing the banquet had been put under a deep sleeping spell. "This is terrible!" Aurora cried.

4 Aurora ran to find Prince Phillip but he was in a deep sleep, too. "The fairies will know what to do," she thought.

5 So Aurora jumped on her horse again and hurried back to the fairies' cottage.

6 Aurora explained what had happened and the fairies hurriedly looked through their spell books, thinking that some enchantress had put a spell on the palace.

7 "Oh, no!" Merryweather suddenly said. "I think it may be all my fault! I put a good luck spell on the banquet and I think I added the wrong potion!"

8 The other fairies were very cross with Merryweather. "You should never do good luck spells," Fauna scolded. "They always go wrong!"

9 "I have an idea of how we can break the spell on the banquet," said Aurora. "We should make a wake-up potion with all the things we need for a banquet."

10 "It's worth a try!" said the fairies. They then cast a spell using all the food in their kitchen to make the potion.

11 The fairies hurried back to the palace with Aurora. First they gave the potion to the Prince and then to all the others.

12 The Prince woke up baffled. "What happened?" he asked. "I'll explain later," said Aurora, "we have a banquet to arrange first."

13 Everyone woke up to find a fantastic banquet waiting for them! "I feel like I've been asleep all afternoon!" yawned the Prince. Aurora shrugged her shoulders and the fairies giggled as everyone began the lovely feast!

The End

Mountain Maze

Aurora is walking through the woodland.

Which path should she take up the mountain to see the good fairies?

Answer: Path b.

Aurora Colouring

Join the dots to complete the butterflies, then finish colouring in this picture of Aurora.

Slipper Brooch

Make and wear Aurora's slipper brooch - it's fit for a princess!

You will need:

purple card

safety scissors

glue

glitter

beads

tape

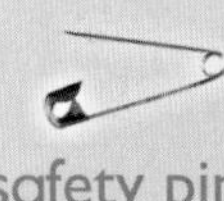

safety pin

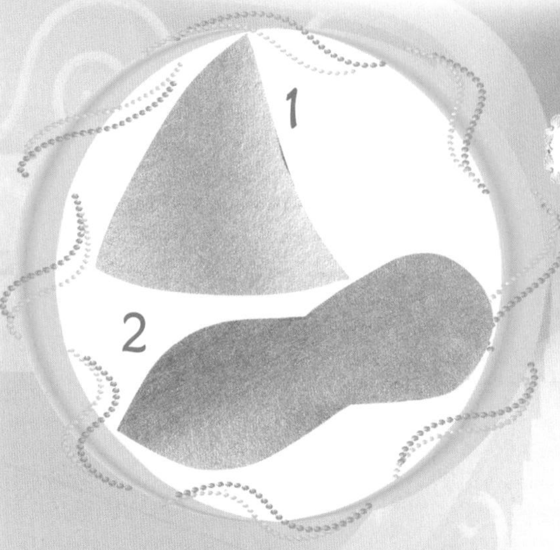

1 To make your slipper, cut out two shapes, like these from a piece of card.

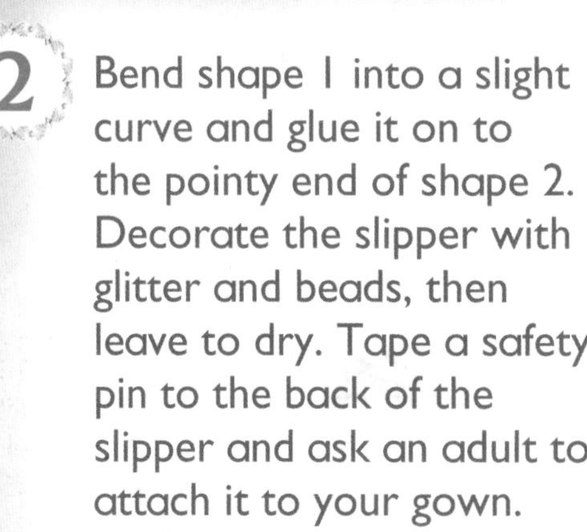

2 Bend shape 1 into a slight curve and glue it on to the pointy end of shape 2. Decorate the slipper with glitter and beads, then leave to dry. Tape a safety pin to the back of the slipper and ask an adult to attach it to your gown.

Memory Game

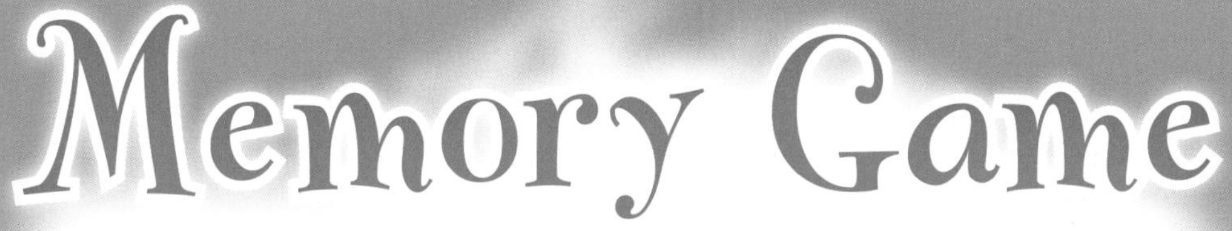

Aurora loves looking after her royal horses.

Play this memory game by covering up the 'horsey' things below, then trying to remember them all.

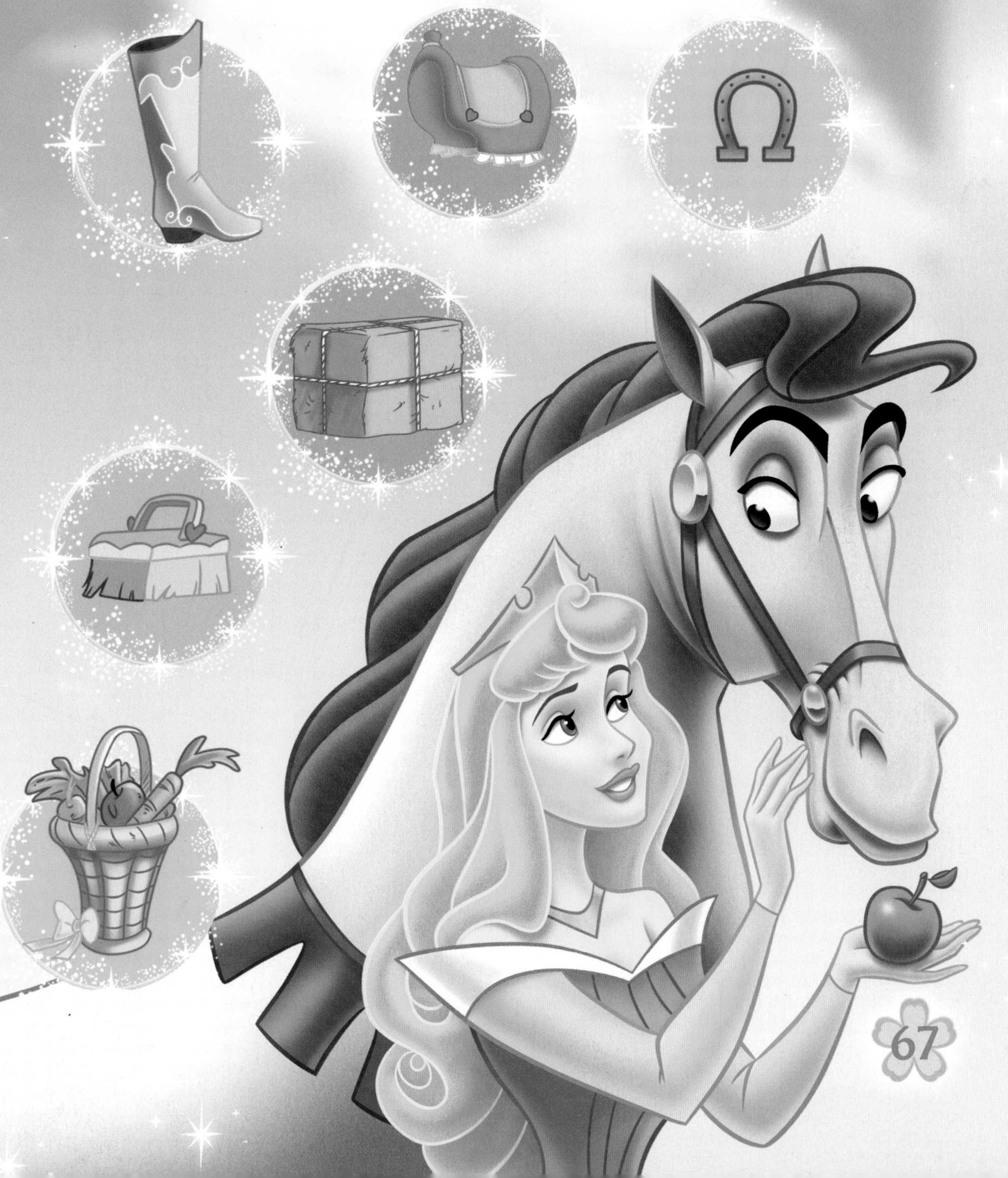

Princess Fun

Now that you have read your Princess Annual, can you match each picture to the correct princess?

Answers: a - Ariel, b - Aurora, c - Cinderella, d - Belle, e - Snow White, f - Jasmine.